WHY THIS IS AN EASY READER

- This story has been carefully written so that it will keep the young reader's interest high.
- It is told in a simple, open style with a strong rhythm that adds enjoyment both to reading aloud and silent reading.
- Only 152 different words have been used, with plurals and root words counted once.
- There is a very high percentage of words repeated. *It is this skillful repetition which helps the child to read independently.* Seeing words again and again, he "practices" the vocabulary he knows, and actually learns the words that are new.

ABOUT THE WORDS IN THIS STORY

- 85 words—*more than half the total vocabulary*—have been used at least three times.
- 30 words have been used at least five times.
- 27 words have been used at least 10 times.
- Some words have been used 49 times.
- This story is especially rich in sound-color words like *Bump, Pop, Bang.* It will encourage phonics readiness and can be used to develop interest in word sounds.

CHOOSE FROM THESE EASY READERS

Will You Come to My Party?
Hurry Up, Slowpoke
Mr. Pine's Mixed-up Signs
The Adventures of Silly Billy
The Secret Cat
Billy Brown Makes Something Grand
Miss Polly's Animal School
The Duck on the Truck

Miss Polly's Animal School

Story by MARY ELTING
Pictures by LISL WEIL
Editorial Consultant LILIAN MOORE

WONDER BOOKS

1107 Broadway, New York 10, N. Y.

Introduction

These books are meant to help the young reader discover what a delightful experience reading can be. The stories are such fun that they urge the child to try his new reading skills. They are so easy to read that they will encourage and strengthen him as a reader.

The adult will notice that the sentences aren't too long, the words aren't too hard, and the skillful repetition is like a helping hand. What the child will feel is: "This is a good story—and I can read it myself!"

For some children, the best way to meet these stories may be to hear them read aloud at first. Others, who are better prepared to read on their own, may need a little help in the beginning—help that is best given freely. Youngsters who have more experience in reading alone—whether in first or second or third grade—will have the immediate joy of reading "all by myself."

These books have been planned to help all young readers grow—in their pleasure in books and in their power to read them.

Lilian Moore
Specialist in Reading
Formerly of Division of Instructional Research,
New York City Board of Education

Kookoo was a kangaroo.

Hop!

Hop!

Hop!

Where was she going?

Slappy was a seal.

Flop!

Flop!

Flop!

Where was he going?

Biff was a bear.

He was going some place, too.

Biff the bear,

and Slappy the seal,

and Kookoo the kangaroo.

Where were they all going?

To a party?

No.

To the dentist?

No.

To the zoo?

No.

They were going to school.

They were going to Animal School,

and Miss Polly was their teacher.

Did she teach them A B C

and 1, 2, 3?

No.

Did she teach them tricks?

Yes! Miss Polly had classes

for the animals you see on TV.

SPECIAL
CLASSES
FOR
T.V.
Miss Polly

"Good morning, class,"

said Miss Polly.

"Today we will learn how to slide.

Look at me."

Miss Polly went up, up, up the steps.

Then she came down

down

down the slide.

"That is the way
to slide on a slide,"
said Miss Polly.
"You do not slide on your head.
You do not slide on your side.
You slide sitting up."

"Come, class," said Miss Polly.

"Come, Kookoo.

Come, Slappy.

Come, Biff.

Slide on the slide."

Kookoo went up the steps. Hop! Hop!

Then Kookoo came down, down,

down the slide.

"Good," said Miss Polly.

"Very good."

She clapped her hands.

Biff clapped, too.

Slappy went up the steps. Flop! Flop!

Then down, down, down came Slappy.

"Good," said Miss Polly.

"Very good."

She clapped her hands.

Biff clapped, too.

"Now, Biff," said Miss Polly,
"you slide on the slide."
Biff went up, up, up.

Biff came down

bump

bump

BUMP!

"Oh, dear!" said Miss Polly.

"That's not the way!"

She did not clap. But Biff did.

He clapped and clapped.

The next day Miss Polly said,

"Come, class.

We will be on TV soon.

Today we will play with the ball.

Look at me."

Miss Polly hit the ball.

Kookoo hit the ball. *Crack!*

Slappy hit the ball. *Whack!*

Smack! The ball hit Biff.

"Oh, dear!" said Miss Polly.

"That's not the way!"

She did not clap. But Biff did.

He clapped and clapped and clapped.

The next day Miss Polly said,

"Come, class.

We will be on TV very soon.

Kookoo and Slappy

will go on the seesaw.

Biff will just clap."

Kookoo and Slappy sat down

on the seesaw.

Up and down they went.

Up and down.

Up and down.

"Good!" said Miss Polly.

"Very good!"

Biff clapped and clapped.

The next day Miss Polly said,

"Come, class.

We will be on TV

very, very soon.

Today we will bounce.

Look at me."

Miss Polly went bounce, bounce.

"Now, Slappy," said Miss Polly,

"bounce with me."

Bounce! Bounce! Bounce!

"Good!" said Miss Polly.

"Very good!"

Biff clapped.

"Now, Kookoo," said Miss Polly,

"bounce with me."

Bounce! Bounce! Bounce!

"Good!" said Miss Polly.

"Very good!"

Biff clapped and clapped.

33

The next day Miss Polly said,
"Come, class.
This is the day we will be on TV."
She got into the Animal School bus.

Miss Polly called,
"Hop in! Flop in! Pop in!"
Away went the bus.
Away went Miss Polly
and Kookoo
and Slappy
and Biff.

Some boys saw

the Animal School bus.

"Where are you going?" they called.

"We are going to be on TV,"

said Miss Polly.

"Come and see."

The boys hopped on their bikes.

And away they went,

behind Miss Polly

and Kookoo

and Slappy

and Biff.

Some girls saw
the Animal School bus.
"Where are you going?" they called.
"We are going to be on TV,"
said Miss Polly.
"Come and see."
The girls put on their skates.
And away they went,

behind Miss Polly

and Kookoo

and Slappy

and Biff

and the boys.

A man in a hole
saw the Animal School bus.
"Where are you going?" he called.
A man on a pole
saw the Animal School bus.
"Where are you going?" he called.
"We are going to be on TV,"
said Miss Polly.
"Come and see."

The man in the hole came up.

The man on the pole came down.

And away they went,

behind Miss Polly

and Kookoo

and Slappy

and Biff

and the boys

and the girls.

Some mothers with babies
saw the Animal School bus.
"Where are you going?" they called.
"We are going to be on TV,"
said Miss Polly.
"Come and see."

The mothers wheeled the babies
along behind Miss Polly
and Kookoo
and Slappy
and Biff
and the boys
and the girls
and the men.

A policeman saw

the Animal School bus.

"Stop!" he called.

Miss Polly stopped the bus.

The boys on bikes stopped.

The girls on skates stopped.

The men and the mothers
with babies all stopped.

"Well!" said the policeman.

"Where do you think you are going?"

"We are going to be on TV,"

said Miss Polly.

"Come and see."

"Well, well!" said the policeman.

"Follow me."

Away they all went,

around the corner

and down the street,

up the steps

and into TV Station WOOF.

"Come, class," said Miss Polly.

"We are on TV.

Slide down the slide."

Kookoo went down.

Slappy went down.

"Good!" said Miss Polly.

"Very good!"

She clapped her hands.

But Biff did not clap.

What was he doing?

Biff went up, up, up.

Biff came down

bump

bump

BUMP!

"Hurray! Hurray!"

cried the boys and girls.

"That's the way!"

And everybody clapped.

"Come, class," said Miss Polly.

"Let's play ball."

Crack! Kookoo hit the ball.

Whack! Slappy hit the ball.

"Good!" said Miss Polly.

"Very good!"

But Biff did not clap.

Biff hit the ball. *Smack!*

What a hit!

The ball went up, up, up.

It came down in Kookoo's pocket.

"Hurray! Hurray!"

cried the boys and girls.

"That's the way!"

And everybody clapped.

"Come, class," said Miss Polly.

"Get on the seesaw."

Kookoo and Slappy went

up and down.

"Good!" said Miss Polly.

"Very good!"

But Biff did not clap.

He got in the way of the seesaw.

Bang! The seesaw came down on *him.*

"Hurray! Hurray!"

cried the boys and girls.

"That's the way!"

And everybody clapped.

"Come, class," said Miss Polly.

"Let's bounce."

Bounce, bounce went Slappy
and Miss Polly.

Bounce, bounce went Kookoo
and Miss Polly.

"Good!" said Miss Polly

"Very good!"

But Biff did not clap.

He gave a hop and came down plop!

That made Miss Polly bounce.

And see where she went!

Miss Polly went up.

Miss Polly went over.

Miss Polly came down PLAP

on the policeman's cap,

then on his lap!

"Hurray! Hurray!"

cried the boys and girls.

"That's the way!"

Everybody clapped for Biff.

And Biff clapped, too!